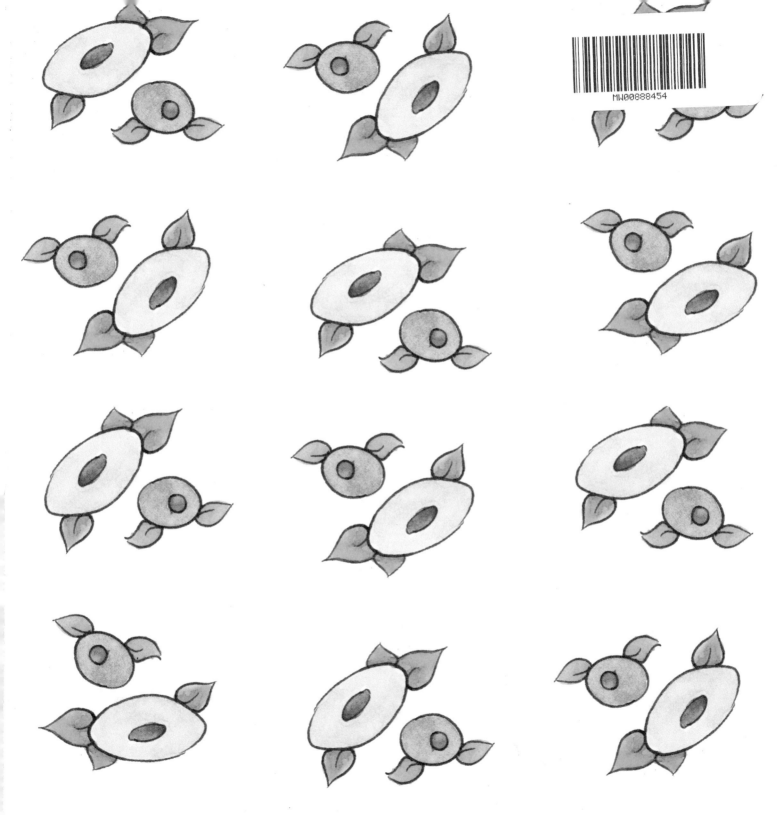

To Janie,
Mary Kate,
and Annie

shybug

by Kevin Ann Planchet

illustrations by Melissa Bailey

"This time I'm going to make it!"

Emmie's mother caught her just as she fell.

"I don't know why my shybug is such a daredevil."

Emmie loved her garden. It was crawling with ladybugs
and butterflies. Sometimes if she was lucky,
one would land on her hand.

She loved her cat Blink and the ladybugs and the butterflies, but it wasn't the same as having someone to play with.

Emmie heard a noise.
She looked over the flowers and saw the top of a head.

She pulled out her magnifying glass to get a better look.

"Hi!" a little girl shouted.
Emmie was so scared she ran into the house.

As Emmie watched the little girl from her bedroom window, she wondered why she'd been so afraid.

That was no way to make a friend.

The next day, Emmie and her mom were clipping flowers from their garden.

"Good morning," a woman called from the next yard. The little girl from yesterday was standing next to her.

"Hello," said Emmie's mother. "You must be our new neighbor."

"This is my daughter, Annie," her mom said.

"Hey, you wanna play?" Annie asked.

Emmie moved closer to her mother and buried her face. "Is she a little shy?" Annie's mother asked.

"Oh yes," Emmie's mother answered.

As their mommies talked, Annie and Emmie looked at each other. Emmie went to the garden and ran her hands across the flowers.

A ladybug landed in her palm.

"How'd you do that?" Annie asked.

Emmie shook her head. "They like my hand," she said in a quiet voice.

"Wow," said Annie. Then her mommy called her home. It was time for lunch.

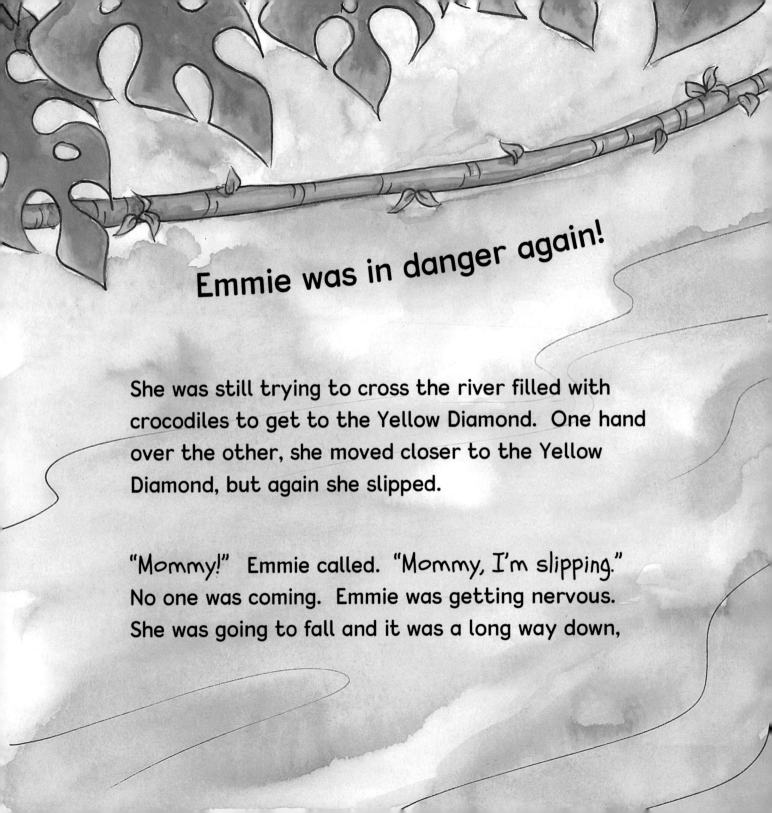

Emmie was in danger again!

She was still trying to cross the river filled with crocodiles to get to the Yellow Diamond. One hand over the other, she moved closer to the Yellow Diamond, but again she slipped.

"Mommy!" Emmie called. "Mommy, I'm slipping." No one was coming. Emmie was getting nervous. She was going to fall and it was a long way down,

but then she felt two
hands under her feet.

Emmie looked down and there was Annie.

"I'll help you!" Annie held Emmie's feet until she made it all the way across.

Emmie grabbed the Yellow Diamond and climbed down to the ground.

"Thank you," Emmie said.

"I heard you calling for help.
What were you doing, anyway?"

"I was crossing the river to get the
Yellow Diamond. I'm filling in the jewels
on my crown."

"That sounds like fun!"

"Do you wanna make a crown, too?"
Emmie asked.

"Let's take a boat!"

the end

About the Author

Though it may be impossible for her current friends to believe, Kevin Ann Planchet was considered a 'shy' child. "Writing was my way to express myself. I've noticed that many reserved people have the desire to be more than their quiet exterior would suggest. Many seem to have these great creative minds through which they can be the extroverts who seem to get everyone's attention."

The character of Emmie is a composite of Kevin's two oldest daughters who were very quiet as children, while the outgoing Annie is actually her outgoing youngest daughter of the same name.

Kevin's first career was as a television reporter, but she has recently completed her Masters in Clinical Mental Health.

"Shybug" is her first children's storybook.

Do you have a shybug?

Then you should resist giving them nicknames or referring to them as such as this is likely to reinforce the shyness. Many people are labeled as shy when in fact they're introverts. Parents sometimes feel the need to draw out a child who seems shy because they think this characteristic may hurt them later in life, but there is a difference between being shy and being an introvert. Introverts aren't necessarily afraid to interact with others. They simply derive satisfaction from pursuits which don't always require spending time with others. Introverted children don't mind playing alone, tend to be thoughtful and are more discriminating when making friends. They are very social with those they are comfortable with. Those who are actually 'shy' tend to be afraid of people and social situations and are more likely to be withdrawn.

Extroverts, on the other hand, thrive on the energy generated by being around others.

What should you do with a child who is an introvert? Don't label them as shy because they're not. Be supportive of the confident self-assured child they are and respect their way of interacting with the world.

What should you do for a child who is shy? Again, don't label them because it reinforces the shyness and may make them feel there is something wrong with them. Be supportive by not forcing them to interact before they're ready. One way to begin tackling true shyness is becoming more comfortable in social situations. This is an area where parents or older siblings can help. Modeling behaviors such as social introductions, shaking hands and being kind and supportive of others can help a shy child to gain confidence in their own skills.

Made in the USA
Monee, IL
14 February 2023

27797146R00021